THE ARRANGEMENT
VOL. 1

H.M. Ward

www.SexyAwesomeBooks.com

Laree Bailey Press

Laree Bailey Press
First Print Edition: Feb 2013

THE ARRANGEMENT

VOL. 1

CHAPTER 1

The night air is frigid. It doesn't help that I'm stuck wearing this little black dress in my crap car. I shiver as I try to keep the engine running at a red light. My little battered car is from two decades ago and stalls if I don't rev the engine while I have my foot on the brake. I'm driving with two feet, in a car that's supposed to be an automatic. The heater doesn't work. If I try to turn it on, I'll get my face blasted with white smoke. It's awesome, in an utterly humbling kind of way. At least the car is mine. It gets me where I need to go, most of the time.

The light flips to green and I botch it. I don't gas the car enough and it shutters and stalls. I grumble and grab for the can of ether. The cars behind me blare their horns.

I ignore them. They can go around me. I grab the can on the seat next to me, kick open my door, and walk around to the hood. I shake the can and spray it into the engine intake. The car will start up as soon as I turn the key now, and I can drive away in shame.

The night air is crisp and filled with exhaust. This road is always busy. It doesn't matter what time of day it is. Angry drivers move around me. Everyone is always in a hurry. It's part of the New York frame of mind. I'm treated to a catcall as a car full of guys blows past me. I flip them the bird and hear their laughter echo as they fade from sight.

Tonight couldn't possibly get any worse. I put the cap on the can of ether. Then it happens. My night takes a one-eighty straight into suckage.

As I drop the hood, it slams shut, and I look through the windshield. "Seriously?" I say at the guy who jumps in my seat. He's wearing a once-blue fluffy coat and hasn't shaved for weeks. He turns the key and my crappy car roars to life. He gasses it and takes off, swerving around me. I stand in the lane staring after him. What a moron. Who'd steal that piece of trash?

Still, it's my car and I need it. After the night I had, I don't want to run after him, but I have to. I need that car. I take off at a full run. My lungs start to burn as I suck in frozen air and exhaust. I run down the shoulder, avoiding trash that's laying in the gutter. My attention is singularly focused on my car. I push my body harder and feel my muscles protest, but I don't hold back. He's getting away.

I manage to run a block when a guy on a motorcycle slows next to me. "That guy stole your car." He sounds shocked.

I can't see his face through the black helmet. It has a tinted visor that covers his face. "No shit, Sherlock," I huff and keep running. My purse is in the car, my only pair of work acceptable heels, my books—awh, fuck—my books. I paid over a grand for those. They're worth more than the car. I run faster. My dress flares around my thighs as my Chucks help me sprint forward. My body doesn't want to do it. The stitch in my side feels like it's going to bust open.

The guy on the bike is annoying. He rolls next to me and flips up his face shield. I glance at him, wondering what he's doing. Biker guy looks at me like I'm crazy. "Are you trying to catch him?"

"Yes," pointing ahead, huffing. There are three lights on this stretch of road before the ramp to get on the parkway. If he hits a red light, the car will stall and I'll get it back. My lungs are burning and it's not like I have time to explain this. My car has already passed the first light. "If he stops, the car will stall."

"You want me to help?" he glances at the car and then back at me.

I stop and nearly double over. Holy hell, I'm out of shape. I nod and throw my leg over the back of his bike, flashing the cars driving past us. I so don't care. Wrapping my arms around his waist, I hold on tight and say, "Go."

"I was going to call the cops, but this works, too." He sounds amused. I hold onto his trim waist and plaster myself against his back. He's wearing a leather jacket, and I can feel his toned body through the supple material. He pulls into traffic and zips through the lanes. The wind blasts my hair and plasters my eyelashes wide open. We bob and weave, getting closer and closer to my car. My heart is racing so fast that it's going to explode.

I see my car. It's passing the second light. Motorcycle man punches it, and the bike flies under the second intersection just as the light changes. I manage not to shriek. My skirt flies up to my hips, but I don't let go of the biker's waist to push the fabric back down.

We're nearly there when the thief catches the third light. The car in front of him stops, forcing the carjacker to stop as well. As soon as he takes his foot off the gas, my car convulses and white smoke shoots out the tailpipe. The engine ceases. The driver's side door is kicked open and the guy runs.

Motorcycle man pulls up next to my car. I slip off the back of the bike, my heart beating a mile a minute. I can't afford to lose this stuff. I'm barely making it as it is. I look at my car. Everything is still there. I turn back to the guy on the bike as I smooth my skirt back into place.

Tucking my hair behind my ear, I say, "Thanks." I must seem insane.

He flips his face shield up and says, "No problem. Does your car always do that?" A pair of blue eyes meets mine and the floor of my stomach gives way. Damn, he's cute. No, not cute—he's hot.

"Get jacked? No, not always."

He smiles. There's a dusting of stubble on his cheeks. I can barely see it because of the helmet. He raises an eyebrow at me and asks, "This has happened before, hasn't it?"

More times than you'd think. Criminals are really stupid. "Let's just say, this isn't the first time I had to chase after the car. So far no one's made it to the parkway. That damn light takes forever and I keep stalling out in the same spot. You'd think I'd figure it out by now, but…" But I'm mentally challenged and prefer to chase after car thieves. I stop talking and press my lips together. His eyes run over my dress and pause on my sneakers, before returning to my face. Great, he thinks I'm mental.

Turning to the car, I grab another can of ether from the backseat and walk around to the front. I dropped the last can somewhere behind me. I pop the hood and spray. I'm so cold that I've gone numb. As I walk back to my door, I shake my head saying, "Who steals a car that barely runs?"

"Do you need any help?" The guy holds my gaze for a moment and my stomach twists. He seems sincere, which kills me. A strange compulsion to spill my guts tries to overtake me, but I bash it back down.

Pressing my lips together, I shake my head, and swallow the lump in my throat. Today sucked. I'm totally alone. No one helps me, and yet this guy did. "No, I'm okay," I lie as I slip into my car and yank the door shut. "Thanks for the ride." I turn the engine over and smile at him. The window is down. It doesn't go up.

"Anytime." He nods at me, like he wants to say something else. All I can see of his face is his crystal blue eyes and a beautiful mouth. He's sitting on a bike that cost more than my tuition. He's loaded and I've got nothing. A pang of remorse shots through me, but I need to go. The haves and the have-not weren't made to mingle. I already learned that lesson once. I don't need to learn it again.

"Thanks," I say before he can ask my name. "I'll see you around." I smile at him and drive away, holding back tears that are building behind my eyes.

It's weird. There are so many shitty people in the world, and on the worst day of my life, I finally find a nice one and I'm driving away from him.

CHAPTER 2

My dress swishes around my knees as I walk down the dorm hallway, toward my room. I'm holding my books under one arm and my heels in the other. My purse is over my shoulder. I have my keys in hand and shove one into the lock and twist. The knob turns and I push, walking forward. The door hits something and I walk into it, smacking my head and dropping everything. It's late and I'm tired. I kick the door with my foot, knowing Amber (the worst roommate ever) blocked the door so I can't get inside.

"Open the door!" I scream and kick it again, but she doesn't open up. I pick my books up off the floor and slip them between the crack in the door. I grab my heels and purse and walk to Melony's room. I knock on the door jam and peek in.

"Hey, how'd your night go?" Melony is leaning toward a mirror, putting on earrings that dangle. They sparkle like sunlight against her dark hair. Her skin is the color of caramel and so are her eyes. She looks like a supermodel. She's wearing a dress that wraps around her narrow waist with a plunging neck line.

"Sucked," I say, laying back on her bed and staring at the ceiling. "I got carjacked again. I really thought thieves were smarter than that."

She turns and looks at me. "Are you hurt?"

"Nah, some guy helped me. I got my car back and the idiot who took it didn't steal anything. He ran when the car stalled. What a dumbass." I press my fingers to my temples, trying to stop the headache that's threatening to tear my brains apart.

"What else happened?" She asks, since having car issues is a normal part of my life. "You seem way out of sorts."

I am way out of sorts. I'm quiet for a moment. I want to tell someone, but Mel has money and I have none. I work my ass off and I still can't get ahead. I swallow hard and say it. "I can't do it anymore, Mel. I can't work and do school. If I don't keep my GPA at a 3.5, I lose my scholarship, but if I don't work—" I groan, covering my face with my arm.

"You can't live. Yeah, I get it." She says, putting away her make-up.

"I don't know what to do. I have a huge test on Monday and I haven't even cracked open the book yet. Then, when the car got jacked—*damn*—all that I could think was that I'm going to fail the test on Monday without my book. I ran down Deer Park Avenue like a lunatic, chasing a stolen textbook."

The bed next to me dips and I realize Mel is sitting there. "You need a new job, honey."

"I know, but it's the same everywhere. Nobody pays enough. I work until I drop dead at night, and I'm still eating Ramen noodles. I can't stand it anymore."

She pats my arm, pulling it away from my face. Her golden eyes meet mine. "Listen, I have to check in at work, take care of some paperwork for tomorrow, and do a few things. My boss is going to be there. You should come and meet her."

I look up at her, "What? And work at a hotel?"

Mel smiles at me funnily, and nods. "Yeah, I mean, why not? It's a good job, it pays great, and the hours are perfect. I work way less than you and make way more."

"That was blunt."

She stands and smoothes her dress, "You need blunt these days, Avery. You're a mess, your car is a death trap, and you're totally alone. A big pay check will fix some of that."

I don't want to go. My body aches. I'm over tired, and going out again sounds like suckage. At the same time, she's right. Money would fix some of my problems. "Since we're being blunt, how much are we talking about?"

"More than enough for you and all your bills. What you earn in a month, I make every weekend." She stares at me with those tiger eyes and I dart upright on the bed.

"Are you serious?" I think Mel's toying with me, but she nods. "What the hell do you do?"

Mel laughs and shakes her head. "Just come. Talk to my boss. If you're a good fit, she'll give you a job. It's what you want, right?"

I push myself up, muttering, "You suck. Fine, I'll come. But I was planning on spending some quality time with Amber tonight."

Melony scoffs and says, "Yeah, right."

CHAPTER 3

Melony drives a sporty black coupe that puts my car to shame. It stops and goes. The windows move up and down. The heater works. *OMFG*, the heater! I could die. I slump back into the leather when the heated seat warms up. "I could live in this car."

"Holy hell, we need to get you off the poor train. Did you hear what you just said?" She looks over at me briefly, before returning her gaze to the road.

I nod and totally don't care. The leather is warm and I have my head tipped back and my eyes closed. "You try living with Amber for a semester and we'll see what crazy crap comes out of your mouth."

"Did she lock you out again?"

"Yeah," I nod. "She's probably having sex with her creepy boyfriend on my couch." I need more Lysol. I cringe thinking about it. How I ended up with such a rank roommate is beyond me. It's like the university asked me all those questions on the roommate application thingie to see if I could manage using a pencil okay. I thought I proved that I could use a pencil when I took my SATs. Guess not.

Melony's little car darts through traffic. We stop at a light and she looks at me. "That guy gives me the creeps."

"Me too. It's like her guy radar only picks out soon-to-be-felons. Listen, my nerves are so frayed, I can't talk about Amber anymore. My frickin' eye is twitching." And it is. The lower right lid is going nuts, blinking for no reason. I press my finger to it, trying not to smear my make-up.

"Fine by me. So," she changes the subject, "are you seeing anyone?"

I laugh in response, and then realize she's really asking, "Uhm, no. With what time? If I'm not at class, I'm at work. If I'm not at work, I'm at class. I don't even have time to sleep. *Am I dating?*" I say mockingly and laugh, shaking my head. My dark hair falls over my shoulders.

"Back off, Cujo. I was just asking, trying to get a feel for things."

"What things? Things that'll never happen this side of hell."

"Sounding a little bitter there, Avery."

I smile weakly at her. She's just trying to help. "Sorry, I didn't mean to snap. Today had to be the worst day of my life. Besides the douche that stole the car, I had the worst customer. He screamed at me forever and then went to my boss. I'm a fucking hostess. Like I have anything to do with his meal?" I press my fingers to my head and lean my elbow on the door. My job is to seat people at a steakhouse. That's it. I have nothing to do with anything else, but this guy wouldn't back off. He seemed to think his night was ruined because of me. By the time he got hold of the manager, somehow everything was my fault. My boss made me look like it was my fault and that sums up my night at work. Absentmindedly, I twist a lock of my hair between my fingers. "It was just one of those days and I'm sick of having them."

"My job is a little unorthodox, but I never have to deal with that shit." Mel shifts in her seat.

I glance at her. "Unorthodox? What do you mean?"

"You'll just have to wait and see." We drive on in silence.

About forty minutes later, we are at a building in Manhattan. A street light floods the sidewalk in front. It looks like an office building. We go inside and ride the elevator up to the seventeenth floor. When the doors open, we're standing in an open space. The room is decorated in browns and beiges with little splashes of color here or there. It looks like an office.

I glance at Mel. "I thought you worked at a hotel?"

"I do, but this is where I check in." She walks past me and turns a corner. I follow her down a hallway. Mel stops in front of an office door. She smoothes her dress, like she's nervous, and knocks. Looking back at me she says quickly, "Don't say anything. Just listen and answer whatever she asks you."

My brows pull together. What the hell am I doing here? Mel is dressed up and from the looks of it, we are in an empty office space. There's no music, no noise. It's totally silent.

"Enter," a female voice says, and Melony pushes the door open. A woman in her early forties sits behind a glass desk. She doesn't look up. "Right on time. Come in and close the door."

Mel's voice cracks, "I brought someone for you to meet." The woman at the desk lifts her eyes and sees me. She immediately shoots daggers at Mel. Mel holds up her hands, explaining, "I didn't say anything. I told her to come and talk to you. I didn't breech my contract, Miss Black. I need to keep this job, but my friend here is in the same position as I was and I thought you were looking for someone new."

I know Mel told me to stay quiet, but I can't. I don't want her to lose her job because of me. "It's all right. I can wait in the car." I turn to leave.

The woman behind the desk rises. Her gaze slips over me quickly. She says to Mel, "Family? Boyfriend? Funding?"

"No to all three," Mel answers.

I stop and stare at the two of them.

"Come with me, Miss. We'll have a chat. Melony can wait here." The woman walks swiftly past me. We move to a table in the back corner of the floor. There is a couch behind us and some more nondescript art on the walls. She sits at the table. It's metal with a glass top. I sit across from her and cross my ankles and pull them under my seat. It feels like an interview.

"Miss Black," I say apologetically, "I'm sorry for disrupting your evening. Mel said this was a good job and I need a good job, so I came."

She nods at me. Miss Black crosses her legs at the knee and leans back in her chair. "How old are you? Twenty-two?" I nod. "Family?"

"Deceased." I still feel the knot in my throat when I say it. I wonder if that'll ever go away.

"What are you attending school for?"

"I want to be a marriage and family counselor when I graduate. I have to finish undergrad and grad school first. I have a very generous scholarship that pays for my classes, fees, and books, but I still have to pay for rent and food."

"You need a job with better pay and fewer hours?" she asks, and I nod. "Are you involved with anyone?"

My eyebrows start to creep up my face. "No, but—"

"Any piercings or tattoos?" Miss Black's eyes sweep over me, like she's looking for them through my dress.

"No," I blurt out, confused. What does it matter if a hotel clerk has tattoos?

"And I'm guessing that's the best dress and shoes you own." I nod, not wanting to answer. It's all I could afford. I thought I looked nice, but I was already at work and then there was the thing with my car. "If you work for us, we expect you to have a certain kind of attire. There are stores where you have to shop. It's not optional. Is that a problem?"

"Only if I can't afford to shop there."

She smiles, "Oh, you'll be able to afford it. Listen. You seem like the type of girl we are looking for—no attachments, driven, hardworking, and ethical." I try not to smile. I still don't know what the job is, but my heart starts to race like I want it very badly. Miss Black takes a card from her pocket and slips it across the table to me. "That is starting salary. It's paid weekly, in cash."

A warning bell is chiming softly in my head before I glance at the card. Cash, why is it cash? Some companies hire extra staff off the books. It shouldn't spook me, but it does when I lift the card. My jaw drops open. "This is more money than I make in a month." Holy shit! Mel wasn't exaggerating.

"I know, and that's just to start. It goes up from there. Those who perform well are paid well."

I stare at the card and the massive number. I've got to be missing something. I look up and ask, "What's my job?"

Miss Black grins and places her palms together. She points her index fingers at me. "Ah, that's where things get tricky. You see, we are in one of the oldest professions in the world—the matchmaking business. Beautiful young women come to us and we take care of them and make sure they're safe. We're selective about our clientele and attempt to match preferences to keep things as pleasant as possible. Now, if—"

My mouth is hanging open. I blink as she speaks, thinking that I must be misunderstanding, but the longer she talks, the clearer things become. I find my voice and squeak out, "You want to be my pimp?"

Okay, today is totally the worst day of my life. I stare at her wide-eyed. "Does Mel know—"

Mel speaks from behind me. "Of course I know. I work here, Avery. I'm a high dollar call girl, if you need the bluntness, and from the look on your face, I think you do." I'm ready to bounce out of my chair and run, but Mel puts a hand on my shoulder and sits next to me. "I know what you're feeling, but hear me out. Miss Black is a madam. It's not the same as whoring yourself out. It's more like matchmaking."

"For money," I retort.

"What's so bad about that? I mean, you get to work a few hours a week, get good pay, and have someone looking out for you. The guys have a background check, are guaranteed drug and disease free. That's better than dating the old fashioned way."

"This isn't dating, Mel!" I stand up, but Mel grabs my wrist and pulls me back into my seat. I'm so annoyed with her. I want to leave, but it's because I'm upset. I can't believe she took me here. I can't believe she does this!

Mel sighs and gives me her annoyed look that's just short of an eye roll. She thinks I'm blowing things out of proportion. "There are different levels of service, Avery. You could just be some guy's arm-candy for the night. No sex. It's your call."

I glance at Miss Black. Her expression is neutral. "Is that true?"

Miss Black nods. "We have different clients with different needs. When you begin working for us, you tell us what you're comfortable with and how far you're willing to go. Limits are set ahead of time so there is no confusion. You have a security device with you at all times and check in here every weekend."

"I—" my mouth is hanging open. Getting paid to be someone's date doesn't sound bad. "I don't know."

Mel explains, "The dates don't pay as much, Avery. But it's a good way to see how good they match you up. I mean, if it's the kind of guy you'd take to bed anyway..." Mel winks at me and then shrugs, like it's no big deal.

I break eye contact with Mel and stare at the table. I'm gripping my hands in my lap so tightly that they're turning white.

Miss Black pushes a sheet of paper in front of me and a pen. "This is a list of things that might occur on a date with a client. You can check off the things you are willing to take part in."

I stare at the sheet. There are normal things—hugs, kisses, pecks, French kissing—and then the list gets more specific: stroking, petting, oral sex, vaginal sex, anal sex, and it keeps going, getting weirder and weirder. There are two columns filled with anything and everything. Fisting? What the hell is that?

I shake my head and push the page back to her. "No." I can't do this. I feel like I'm standing on the slippery slope and about to fall down, ass first.

Miss Black eyes me for a moment, like she knows me. "How experienced are you, Avery?"

I freeze, and my shoulders straighten. I turn to her slowly. My answer must be written across my face, because Miss Black smiles at me with that smile people have when they discover something serendipitous.

Miss Black hands me another card. This one is black with white letters. My reflex is to take it. "*That* also has its own set of rules and prices." I squirm under her gaze. I wonder how she can tell. I hold the card in my hand without looking at it, heart pounding.

Mel isn't following, "What has its own rules?"

"Your friend is a virgin," Miss Black says, pleased.

CHAPTER 4

My face flames red, but I can't move. I flip the little black card over and look at it, expecting the number to be smaller, but it isn't. It's bigger, with a lot of zeros. I don't understand. Glancing up at Miss Black, I ask, "Why is it more?" I thought it'd be less. Who'd want to pay to fuck a virgin? I don't know what I'm doing, like at all.

Miss Black tilts her head to the side. "Supply and demand. There are very few women your age with everything still intact. Some men like being the first. They want a more drawn out experience, so it costs more. Combine that with a lack of virgins and you are a rare commodity."

Oh boy. I'm a rare commodity. I don't blink. I just stare at her. It's like I've fallen into a parallel universe or something.

Mel blurts out, "Why didn't you tell me?"

Mel looks at me like I've been living a double life for the past few years. It irks me, since she really is living a double life. I had no idea she was doing this. I don't want to talk about it now, either. "It's not the kind of thing that comes up, okay."

Mel stumbles over her words and finally spits out, "How?"

Miss Black speaks for me, "She never found the right guy, is my guess. Avery's been too busy with life, trying to survive. A guy complicates things, adds more danger, and more uncertainty."

I feel numb. That was exactly why. If I got pregnant, robbed, infected, or anything else, then I'd be totally screwed. I stare at the floor. "There's no room for it. If I make a mistake…"

Miss Black nods. "I understand. Don't make a decision now. Think about it and let me know. My number is on the back of the card. I need to check Melony's stats and you girls can be on your way."

"Have you done it?" I blurt out as I look up at her. I don't know why I asked, but I did. Miss Black turns back to me and nods slowly. "Do you regret it?"

"There are some things I wish I'd done differently, but it was my own fault. The job was great, Avery. My regret is that I held onto the job too long and the result was letting the right guy slip away."

Mel whispers to me, "We can't date when we're working here."

Miss Black shakes her head, and looks at Mel. "Come on. Let's get your stats."

Mel walks to a scale and stops in front of it. She turns once showing her dress off to Miss Black. "It ties at the waist." She pulls the string and slips out of the dress. Mel is wearing a navy bra and panty set with matching garters and thigh highs. She slips out of her shoes and steps on the scale. Miss Black measures her waist, breasts, and hips, and writes the numbers down.

Mel turns to me, "They regulate everything."

"Would I have to do this for the dating service?" They both nod.

"It helps us keep you in shape and pair you up with the right man. We want our clients to be happy. Most of them want a specific kind of woman." Miss Black answers me as she fills in information on Mel's chart.

"Specific numbers?" I ask, shocked.

"Specific ratio. It gives a good indication of curves. The clients will never see your measurements, of course. That's just for us." Miss Black eyes me, while Mel pulls her dress back on. "Why don't you come in with Mel tomorrow. I'll bring the—"

I shake my head. I've made up my mind. The moment of insanity has passed. There's no way I can do this. "No, that's okay. This is too much for me."

Miss Black leans in. "One guy, for one month and you'd be set for the year. It's just one guy, Avery. Think about it."

I don't need to think about it. This isn't for me. "No, but thanks anyway." I say. I flick a glance at Mel and want to strangle her. What was she thinking, bringing me here? And what the hell is she thinking, doing this? I look down and bite my tongue.

Miss Black is talking to Mel about her next date and walks toward a bookshelf on the wall. She lifts a photo album and walks back to the table. Mel sits next to me. I grab my phone and pretend to tweet something. Mel's spine straightens. She knows I'm going to chew her out when we're alone. Damn right, I am.

Miss Black says to Mel, "There are a few new clients who haven't been entered into the database yet. You know how we are with these things. Everything is private, but it takes time. Anyway," she says, putting the thick book on the table, "I'll show you his paper file. This'll be destroyed later."

Mel scoots closer, so she can see. When Miss Black flips open the thick binder something flutters to the floor. It's a picture and some notes that are written too poorly for me to read. I lean over and pick them up. When my fingers touch the picture, I freeze. Those eyes, that face. A chill runs down my spine. It's the guy from earlier tonight, the one on the motorcycle. I pause there, afraid to touch it. A rush of feelings swirl through me and pool in my stomach. I can't swallow.

"Avery, what's wrong?" Mel asks, noticing how I've gone rigid.

"Nothing." I sweep up the papers and the picture and hand them back to Miss Black. When I touch the photograph, I think of how it felt to wrap my arms around his waist. Hell, I already wrapped my thighs around his hips. My face flames red at the thought and the two women chuckle, like they know what I'm thinking. I push the papers across the table toward Miss Black.

The corners of her mouth twitch with amusement. She senses the chink in my armor. "This is a new client. I met him this morning and he was interested in finding someone to take under his wing, someone with little experience, someone with soft dark hair and even darker eyes—someone like you."

I smile too widely and shake my head. Butterflies are ambushing my stomach and trying to fly up my throat. I move too much and practically shake my brains out of my head. "I'm not interested." I try to hide my nerves, but the fact that this guy made me melt before I saw the picture undercuts me. I cross my arms over my chest and lean back in the chair, locking my jaw.

"Very well," Miss Black says, no longer looking at the guy's picture. She turns to Mel and pulls out a few pages. There are a lot of pictures of the guy and his preferences are noted.

I tune out what they say. I don't realize it, but I'm staring at the upside down picture of motorcycle man. He seemed so normal, so nice. What's he doing at a place like this? If he asked me out, I would have said—*stop lying to yourself, you would have said no*. I wouldn't have given him a chance, and why? Because I don't have time for stuff like this. I won't start something that I can't finish.

My eyes fixate on his face. Startling blue eyes look back. A dusting of stubble lines his jaw, dark like the sexy hair covering his head in thick waves. It sweeps across his forehead, like it's just a little too long. I want to touch it, and push the hair back. Those eyes are too amazing to conceal. My heart is pounding and I'm lost in thought, rethinking the encounter with him earlier tonight, wondering why he'd come here, when Mel pokes me in the shoulder.

"Hello? Earth to Avery?" I snap my gaze from the picture and look at her. "Time to go." Mel stands and grabs her purse.

Miss Black extends her hand to me, "It was a pleasure to meet you."

I nod, and shake. "It's been.." I stare at her, and can't think of anything to describe how it's been.

Miss Black breaks the awkward pause and says, "I did the same thing. So did, Melony, if it makes you feel better. Neither of us thought we'd do it. We both said no at first." Miss Black smiles weakly at me. The handshake stops and before I have a chance to turn away, she says, "We both changed our minds."

I smile at her, completely and total certain. "I won't be changing my mind about this."

I turn away and follow Mel down to her car. I had no clue how wrong I was.

CHAPTER 5

Mel stalks to her room. There's a frosty silence between us. It's nearly 2:00am by the time we get back to the dorm. We pass my door first. I move to unlock it, but when I jab my key in and turn the knob, the door smacks into the couch. Again.

"Damn it, Amber! Open the fucking door!" I'm about to lose my mind. It's the middle of the night. There's no one to report her to, and I am not sleeping in the hallway.

Mel stops a few paces away and turns back when she hears me yell. Her voice is quiet. "Come stay with us. You can beat the crap out of Amber in the morning." She doesn't wait for me to cave and follow her back to her room. I watch Mel's long curvy form walk down the hall and wonder if I know her at all. She's a goddamn prostitute. How did I miss that? Am I that naïve? I suck in a breath of air and let it out in a rush.

Running my hand through my hair, I push it back from my eyes and sulk down the hallway after her. She opens the door in silence. I follow her into the room and close the door quietly, assuming her roommate is already asleep, but the room is empty. We both live in the west tower at the far end of campus. It's the cheapest dorm and the one farthest from everything.

Mel picks up a note next to the lamp after she turns it on. The little room is a photocopy of mine, minus my hideous roommate, Amber the skank. The walls are eggshell white with an industrial tile floor. Mel decorated it more poshly than I did. I could never afford the pretty curtains and thick throw rug that covers the floor. All the throw blankets, lights, and pictures make it feel like a home. My room doesn't feel like that. It feels like the prison cell of a sociopath. Amber covered her half with sparkly crap and my half remains empty, barren, like my life.

Mel reads the note and puts it down. "She's out for the night." There's an awkward pause that makes my mouth fill with cotton. I feel like I should apologize, but I don't want to. She took me to fill out an application to be a hooker.

Mel presses her lips together and looks at me. "I didn't mean to…" she closes her eyes and shakes her head. Pressing a finger to her temple, she says, "I didn't mean to upset you and I sure hope that we can still be friends." She works her jaw after she carefully says each word and stares at me.

"I'm pissed, but I'm not stupid. Why wouldn't we be friends anymore?" I feel a tug in my gut, a warning that I might actually lose her. It makes me step further into the room. I can't lose her. She's my best friend and as close to family as I'll get.

"You've got that look on your face. The one that says condemnation, damnation, and all those other nations where sleeping with a guy is frowned on and followed up with a swift banishment with brimstone." Her hands move as she speaks, flying through the air. She's really worried.

I sigh and rub the heel of my hand against my eyes. "Mel, oh my God, that's *not* it. You walked me into a job interview to be a hooker. I thought I was applying to be a hotel clerk. They're kind of different, in case you didn't notice. You frickin' blindsided me, that's all." That's all, like that's nothing major. My best friend is a hooker. My shoulders slump forward. I don't want to fight anymore. I'm exhausted and I have to get up early to study, since I have to work tomorrow night. I sit down hard on a fluffy hot pink chair and pull a blanket over my lap.

Mel sits across from me on her bed. She pulls off her shoes and stockings, as she speaks. "You wouldn't have come if I told you what it was, and I don't know if you've noticed this or not—but you're screwed. If you get one C, just one, you're totally fucked. No more scholarship, no more college, poof! It's gone. You're walking the line already in Psych. You can't fail Monday's test. It kills your wiggle room, and you'll have to pull straight A's for the rest of the semester. You know you can't do that working as much as you do. This is an upper level class, Avery. You're almost done. It would suck to blow the whole thing now."

I stare blankly at the wall as she speaks. I already know all this, but hearing it still stings. I don't look at her. I feel more desperate every day. I can't handle this on my own, but I am on my own. There's no one to help me when I fall flat on my face, which seems like it's going to happen soon. I'm on the downward slope and picking up speed. If things don't change, I'll crash. I can't think about it. I push the thoughts away, unable to deal with the repercussions.

"How'd you end up working there?" I ask, still feeling uneasy, picking at the fringe of the blanket on my lap.

Mel looks at me cautiously. "I was doing what you are doing and falling behind. I'm not losing my scholarship. It's my only way out of that hell hole.

When I came here, I said that I wouldn't go back. Come hell or high water, I have kept that promise to myself."

Determination burns in Mel's eyes. My eyes just feel tired. I look at her, not understanding how Mel could do it. At the same time, I hear it in her voice— she can't go back. I have nothing to go back to, but still... I can't do what she does. I want my first time to be with someone I love. I never, even for a second, thought about selling sex.

My mind goes in several different directions. I doubt she follows me when I say, "I admire you, you know. You have more guts in one eyelash than I have in my entire body. I'm going down in flames and I can't stop it."

"Yes, you can," she says, her voice filled with empathy. "Listen, Avery, you don't have to do what I did, but you have got to do something. We both see the crash and burn racing up on you. Change something. Take control of your life so it doesn't happen."

"You think you can control life? What are you, new?" I shake my head and tuck my feet under my butt. "Life is random crap that happens. You can't control it."

"No," Mel says, her voice full of conviction, "Your life is what you make it, and right now you're letting a good life slip away. This is a good chance,

Avery. Maybe it's not the way you thought things would be, but working for Miss Black has been a godsend for me. I would have lost my scholarship and had to crawl home. No one said I'd make it. They thought I'd burn out and fail. That gave me more conviction to stay and fight. I'm not living like them. I refuse."

Mel folds her arms over her chest. Her family abused the crap out of her. She was battered, neglected, and selling dime bags before she was 12 years old. Mel left her family as soon as she was old enough, and cut them off without looking back.

Meanwhile, it seems that all I can do is look back. If my parents were alive, this wouldn't even be a consideration. I'd be living at home, eating my mom's meatballs, and having my dad fix my car when it acts up. Instead, my life took an unexpected turn and here I am, fending for myself before I'm ready. I'm so not ready, but it's sink or swim time and I'm drowning.

My voice is small when I speak. "I can't let some guy have me and then take the money off his nightstand. I can't get paid for sex. I just can't. I know you mean well, but—"

"The guy doesn't pay you, Miss Black does. It feels like a date, Avery, a really good date. And if you took the deal they offered you, it'd be better than that. You'd have insta-boyfriend and he'd walk you through everything, Miss Virgin, which is way better than guessing," Mel smiles sheepishly, like she's thinking of something embarrassing. "I don't know. It just doesn't seem that bad to me. It sounds like dating made easy… and by the way, here's some money."

I smile at her. "You make it sound easy."

"It's easier than dating. You never know if the guy's lying or where his thingie's been. And he's just trying to get into my pants anyway. This is easier." Mel smiles at me.

I laugh. "Thingie? Is that the professional terminology taught to you by the prestigious hooker co-op?"

"Co-op. Cute. Real cute."

Shrugging, I grin, saying, "I try."

"No you don't. You're just naturally wholesome, like butter. In little quantities you're all right, but large doses—"

"You are so gross!" I throw a pillow at her as she finishes the sentence.

We talk about random things after that. I don't want to entertain the idea of working for Miss Black, but it keeps jumping into my mind like a demented bunny rabbit. I start to doze off and *spring!* there it is again. And the question that bothers me most is this:

Would it be so bad?

I see those blue eyes and think maybe not, but I can't cross that line. Something inside me holds me back.

CHAPTER 6

I'm waiting at the stop light from hell the next night, trying to keep the car running. It's cold. My breath makes little white clouds in the car as I breathe. I'm wearing an ugly old sweater over my dress, with my sneakers tied onto my feet. I watch the RPMs and give it more gas. I feel the car shake and know that it's going to stall out if the light doesn't change soon.

I stare at the light, willing it to change. "Change already! Change, you rat bastard, change!"

The light remains red. The car shudders and dies. Exasperated, I slam my head on the steering wheel. The stoplight flips to green and the honking starts. I mutter curses as people move their cars out of my lane and go around me. I reach behind me and grab a can of ether from the back seat. Throwing the car door open, I march around to the front. This is the last can and I don't get paid for three days. Damn it.

Lifting the hood, I spray the engine and sigh. FML. I can't stand this. I didn't get to study as much as I needed, work sucked, and now this. It's part of my life. This car symbolizes my life, the damn whole thing. I stare blankly at my car as my insides twist with grief.

I hear his voice before I notice the bike. "So, do you come here often?"

When I slam the hood, I see those sapphire eyes and that boyish smirk. Motorcycle man winks at me. My heart races when I think of his picture, of what he wants, and that he could do it to me if I took that job. He's wearing the helmet, so I can't see his hair, but I'm sure it's him.

"You know it. This is my favorite place." I round the car and intend on driving away. The guy on the bike moves out of traffic and waits for me to start the car. I turn the key and engine makes an awesome noise, but it won't turn over. I try again and again, muttering, "This can't be happening."

I try one last time and know that it won't start. I have a test at 8:00am. It's going to take hours to get a tow truck, which I can't afford. I lean my head against the steering wheel to gain some composure before freak out tears flood from my eyeballs. My head lightly brushes against the horn. The thing blares like I smacked my face on it. I flinch back, jerking my hands away, but the horn continues to wail. I sit there for a moment and blink before hysterical laugher works its way up my throat.

I kick the door open and get ready to push the car out of the lane. As I throw my weight against the metal between the door and the frame of the car, Motorcycle man appears next to me. I feel him there, pushing with me. The car is instantly lighter and it rolls forward, horn blaring. I cut the wheel and turn it into a parking lot. I'm wondering if I ran his bike over. I don't see it and I sure as hell can't hear anything but the horn.

When we get the car into a parking spot, the guy steps past me, pulls the emergency brake, and disappears under the hood. Suddenly the horn dies, and then the hood drops. "That's better," he says.

I'm rubbing my arms. Nerves creep up my stomach and try to choke me. "Thanks."

"No problem. Glad I was here."

I glance up at him. "Me too. I mean, I'm glad I didn't have to push the car out of traffic by myself."

He's smiling at me. I let my eyes slip over his body and try not to drool. My God, he's beautiful. "Like what you see?"

My face flames red as my eyes widen. "Wow, you're blunt."

"Sometimes it pays off, and other times…" he shrugs.

"Other times what?"

"Other times it gets me smacked." He smiles wickedly at me before lifting his helmet off. That dark hair is all rumpled like he's been rolling around in bed. I try not to let him get to me, but there's something there, some carnal attraction.

"Mmmm. Well, you were out of reach." I smirk at him and wonder what I'm doing. Something's wrong with this guy. He wants a virgin hooker. That's like the biggest oxymoron ever.

He laughs. "What's that look?"

"Yeah, it's the *why is this guy here when ever my car breaks down*, look."

"Hmmm, and I thought I left my crazy stalker helmet at home. Is this the one with the warning label?" He flips his helmet around and pretends to look at it. The corners of my mouth pull up, but I try not to smile. I don't want to react to him. I want him to walk away and leave me alone. No, that's a lie. I want to know what's wrong with him, why he wants a hooker.

I can't help it, I laugh. "You forgot to take your meds, dude."

"Is it that obvious? And here I thought I was just being a good citizen, stopping and helping the crazy girl with the spray-start car." He's smiling at me and steps closer. My heart tries to jump up my throat and run down the street. I can't swallow. I can't breathe. When did it get so hot out here?

"Stalking isn't usually considered being a good citizen, in fact, it's kind of frowned upon." I have no idea what I'm saying. I just want to hear his voice and see that smile.

He presses his hand to his heart like I've wounded him. "Is it, now? I thought helping a damsel in distress was chivalry."

I laugh at that. "Chivalry? I think you mean being creepy."

"You know what I think, spray-start car girl?" He steps closer to me and looks down into my eyes. "I think you're enjoying this conversation."

"I have no idea what you're talking about Motorcycle Man. Where is your bike, by the way?" He jabs his thumb in the air back to the intersection where I stalled. The bike is fine. "Thank God. I thought it was stuck under my fender."

"That bike would have eaten your fender."

"Would it now?" A gust of cold air blows my hair away from my face.

Motorcycle man's eyes drink me in before he nods. "Indeed." His voice is rich. It slips over me and

I shiver. Our eyes lock and I can't look away. We stare at each other even though we've run out of things to say. The wind whips a curl over my lips. He lifts a hand and tucks the hair behind my ear. After a second he breaks the trance. "We need to call you a tow truck."

"No," I say a little too strongly. He glances at me. I explain, "I'll come get it tomorrow. It just needs to sit. I probably flooded the engine." It's the only thing I can think to say.

Instead of calling me on it, Motorcycle man nods and says, "Then, let me take you home."

I stare at him for a moment, a wisp of a smile skirts across my mouth. "Ah, but then you'll know where I live, and I don't think we should encourage your stalker habits."

"I can be more of a bastard, if you like. I could drive away and leave you here in the cold, but then I wouldn't be around to reap the rewards of my actions. Let's just cut to the chase, Miss…"

"Smith," I lie, not wanting to give him my name.

He gives me a crooked grin, like he knows that's not my name, "Very well, Miss Smith. How about I take you to the general area you'd like to be dropped off. If that's too creepy, I could call you a cab, but you're likely to get someone way creepier than me." He's smiling at me, and it's a perfect smile.

Looking into his eyes, I say, "Tell me your name."

He looks surprised for a second and then says, "Mr. Jones."

The corner of my mouth tugs up slowly. He's lying. We're both demented lunatics because we both seem to like it. "Mr. Jones, will you please drop me off at Frist and Lexington?"

"By the college?"

I nod. "Yup."

"No problem. I was headed that direction anyway."

"You were not," I say and follow him to his bike. Suddenly I notice my dress and sneakers, and my total lack of the correct kind of clothing. The dress is sheer. It'll blow up to my waist again. Plus I have no jacket and the weave on this sweater is so lose you could throw a rock through the holes.

As if he can read my thoughts, Mr. Jones opens a saddle bag and tosses me a jacket. It's some kind of microfiber. I slip it on. It's thin, but it's warm. I swing my leg over the back of the bike and tuck my skirt in as tightly as possible. He feels me moving around after starting the bike. "You ready?"

"Hold on. I'm trying to get my skirt to stay up."

He laughs. "That sounds so wrong."

"Yeah, well, I bet you wish I was flashing you right now instead of all the cars driving by."

He looks over his shoulder at me before flipping his visor shut and says, "I can feel your thighs around me. I'm good."

Before I can say anything, the bike jerks forward and cuts into traffic. I cling to his back and tighten my knees against his sides. Bastard.

CHAPTER 7

Mr. Jones slows the bike in a semicircle at the front of campus. Half frozen, I slip off the back and jump up and down trying to warm myself. The skin on my face and legs is totally numb. I can't feel anything.

He lifts his helmet off and says, "Sorry I didn't have pants."

"If you had spare pants, I don't think we could be friends." I shiver and rub my hands over my arms.

He smiles at me, sets the helmet on his seat, and walks over to me. My heart slams into my ribs and I stop jittering like a Chihuahua. The way he does it is smooth, slow. Each step toward me makes my heart pound harder. His eyes lock with mine and make me melt. The playful smile on his lips makes me want to know him more. Before he does it, I know I want his arms around me, so that when they slip around my waist, it feels good. He's so warm and smells like heaven. His scent hits me hard and I can't help but inhale deeper. His fingers brush against my cheek as he slips his hand into my hair.

Pulse pounding violently, I remain transfixed by his eyes. He lures me in, so slowly, and right before our lips touch, he stops. His dark lashes lower and he hesitates. I feel his breath slip across my lips in a warm rush. He breathes, "Sorry," and pulls away.

Every inch of my body wanted that kiss. I don't know what happened. I blink and look away. His hands slip from my body and the cold air makes me shiver. "For what?" I ask, unable to let it go. I don't want to beg for a kiss, but I can't let it slide.

His eyes flick up. He holds my gaze for a moment and a surge of heat passes between us. I want to reach out and pull him into my arms. The way he looks at me, the way his shoulders slump forward, makes him look beaten, like he needs me. The reasonable part of my brains asks, *Are you insane?* She's so annoying. It's just a kiss and yes, I am. Shut up.

He smiles sadly at me and kicks something on the ground with his boot. "Nothing, it's just that I don't even know your name, and then I try to kiss you after you had the worst day of your life. That's kind of scummy of me."

"The worst day of my life was yesterday, if you're basing your decisions facts." I step toward him, wondering if this is a game and that I'm being played. "And my name is…" Rationality says not to tell him, but I like him. He's more than attractive, there's more there. "Avery."

He looks at me and says, "Sean."

I smile, saying, "Sean Jones, chivalrous motorcycle man with only one pair of pants."

He laughs and I smile in response. I step closer to him and look up into his crystal blue eyes. I take his jacket in my hands and pull him to me. Sean doesn't hesitate this time. When I press my lips to his, he kisses me back. It's so sweet and gentle that I want to die. That kiss makes every part of me feel light, like I'll float away. When his hands find my face, he holds me gently, trailing his finger along my jaw and back into my hair. It's a sweet kiss, a chaste kiss, but it leaves me breathless and wanting more.

Sean steps away from me and reaches for his helmet. "Your kiss is addictive, Avery Smith."

I smile at the use of my fake last name, and at the way he says he likes my lips. "Likewise."

I don't know what I think will happen next, but when Sean turns to leave, my heart falls into my shoes. That's it? He's leaving? I don't get it. The only thing that I can think is that he doesn't want me. Dejected, I step up onto the sidewalk. I turn away from him and start to head toward my dorm.

"Miss Smith," he calls after me and I turn around. A gust of wind catches my hair, making the long dark strands streak like inky streamers against the sky. "It's been a delightful evening." He grins at me before flipping his visor shut. The engine on his bike roars and he's gone.

I don't mean to, but I watch him leave until the taillight is lost in traffic.

What am I doing? I'm infatuated with a guy that wants hookers, rather than women. *Women can be hookers too, genius.*

I have no idea what I think about anything anymore. My life is changing. I feel the telltale tilt as my world shifts to one side. The question is, what am I going to do about it?

CHAPTER 8

"Technically, you passed," Mel says to me as we walk toward our next class. She looks sleek, with her dark suit and short skirt. I'd die to have her shoes. They're so cute.

Mentally, I feel like my brain already vacated my body. I sense it happening—I'm switching to survival mode. Funny, I thought I was already in survival mode, but I wasn't. Not fully. The thick air, the unblinking eyes, the way the wind stings as it whips by my face. I remember how this feels, how my entire body seems to shut down just to make it to tomorrow. I'm not breathing. My lips are pressed into a thin line and my jaw locks. I feel Mel's hand on my shoulder, but it doesn't register beyond that. I hear her voice, but all I can think is that I'm screwed. If I lose my scholarship, I have no home—no future.

I ask the question before I think about it, "Do morals matter?"

Mel raises a perfect eyebrow and glances at me. "Are we having a philosophical discussion here, or are you asking something more specific?"

"What's their purpose? I always thought morality was there to guide us, to help us. What happens when it doesn't help? What happens when it's just in the way?" I don't wait to hear the answers. I already know what morals are for. I took that class. I know my heart and my mind. I can't sell my body. It's fundamentally wrong, but there's a tiny thought that brushes through my head when I consider it that seems to think surviving is all that matters. There's part of me that's Machiavellian and doesn't care what the cost is to get what I want, but is that so bad? I just want to live. I want the life that I had before. It wasn't much, but it was mine. Now, it's gone. I swallow hard and take off running. I run away from Mel and away from class. I run away from everyone and everything.

I need to think. I knew this was happening. For the past few weeks things have gotten harder. My life is slipping away. I can feel it shifting beneath my feet like sand. I'm sick of it. I'm sick of everything. I hear Mel's voice behind me, but she doesn't chase after me. No one does. I'm alone. In a city of millions, on a campus of thousands, in a courtyard of hundreds—I'm alone.

Breathless, I clutch my books to my chest and run to the other side of campus, away from the dorms, away from my books and classes. I stop at the base of the tunnel that runs under the highway. I hate going this way. The cement tunnel stretches under the street to keep kids from becoming road-kill, but it creeps me out. I enter the tunnel and walk down the sidewalk, listening to the sound of car engines running and horns blaring.

I turn the corner at the end of the underpass and am back out on the street. I walk a little further and head into a diner, and grab a booth. A waiter brings me a cup of coffee before I open my books and look at the test. A big fat 69 is written in red ink on the cover, a D. This grade will destroy me. It wasn't that I don't understand what I read; it was that I didn't have time to commit the material to memory.

I stare at the paper, at the numbers and the rounded sweep of the prof's handwriting. I feel like the answers are here. One class stands between me and my future. One class. One grade. One professor.

My fingers twiddle the corner of the page as I stare at it. After all this time, this is what breaks me—a fucking grade. It's not fair. Life's not fair. It's hard, too hard to manage alone. I slip the test out of the way, moving it next to me, and grab onto the coffee cup. I watch people as they walk in and out, wondering if their life is as fucked up as mine. I wonder if things turned out remotely the way they'd planned.

No matter what I choose, I have a home until the summer. Then, I can appeal when they pull my scholarship, but the university usually doesn't grant appeals. The scholarship is too valuable. They'd rather grant the money to someone who doesn't work, someone who has family to help them pay for everything else. I don't have those things.

I stare into space as I sip my coffee. Miss Black's words echo in my head, *It's only one guy.* And I've met him. It's a hot guy with quite kissable lips.

A familiar voice startles me. "Cutting class? Ooooh, you're gonna get in trouble." Marty Masterson, slides into the booth opposite me, still grinning. He's my lab partner this semester and is nosy beyond belief. I quickly slap my hand over my test and try to slip it off the tabletop, but Marty already saw it. He snatches it before I can say anything. His eyes flash with concern as he looks up at me. "Avery, holy crap. Are you all right? What happened?" He holds the paper in his fist and questions me like a parent would.

I snatch it back and shove it next to me in the booth. "Work happened. Life happened. Sometimes shit happens."

"But you don't get any do-overs," he looks concerned. Marty takes off his scarf and puts it next to him. He's wearing a corduroy jacket and looks like he belongs in the 70's with that mop of a haircut. But he's kind to me and always has been. I just can't stand the look on his face, like he pity's me, like I'm already dead. "Avery..."

"I'm already aware of my screwedness, so unless you have something else to talk about—" Socially oblivious is a good way to describe Marty. He seems like he's gay, but hasn't said anything about it. I haven't seen him with another guy or a girl. He touches too much, but it never feels sexual. He seems like a large old lady in some ways. Like the exaggerated way he moves his head and his hands when he talks.

"I don't, but you can't seriously think about tossing me back out in the cold without a cup of joe?" He smiles at me and flags the waiter to order a cup.

"I suppose not."

As the waiter comes over and pours black coffee into a bone white mug, Marty looks at me with pity in his eyes. "Stop it." I say.

"Stop what? Stop fretting for you? Because that's not going to happen. What are you going to do? Quit work? That's what you have to do, right?"

"I can't eat if I quit. As it is, this coffee is out of my price range." I slouch and sink back into the seat.

"I'll buy your coffee, but honey, you can't lose that scholarship. Next to nobody gets it and no one ever keeps it. The GPA requirements are insane. It looks good on paper, but holding those numbers for the entire length of your degree plan is—"

"Insane. I know, but it is what it is." My Dad used to say that. I smile weakly and look at my coffee. It's black. No sugar. No cream. 100% bitter, like my life.

"What are you going to do?"

I shrug. "No idea. I guess I'm not cut out for this." I don't mean it, but I feel like taking a pity trip, but Marty doesn't let me.

"No sir. Don't you dare start talking like that. You're nearly done. It makes no sense to give up now. Maybe you can shift your work schedule to give you later hours? You can study in the morning and—"

"And never sleep. Yeah, I tried that. It's not a good long term plan. There's nothing…" my words fall off my tongue. I stare at Marty, wondering what he would do—if he would take a job like the one I was offered if it would save him. "Marty, how far would you go if you were me? I mean, if there was a way for me to stay here, but it was…" my lips twitch as I search for the right word.

He doesn't even let me finish. "I'd tell you to do whatever it takes. Hell, sell pot to freshmen if you have to, but don't leave. Once you leave, there's no way you're coming back. If you give this up, it means you settled for a life you didn't want." He looks at me oddly, his thick hand strokes his stubbled chin. Marty has that linebacker look with thick blonde hair and buttery brown eyes. Basically, he's a teddy bear with uber good perception.

I don't look at him. I stare at the table and wish there was something else that I'd not thought of. After a moment of silence, I ask, "So, you'd understand if I did something stupid to stay here?"

He smirks, "As long as you don't get caught."

Maybe I'm asking the wrong person? I look at him for a moment before saying, "So, you'd do anything, as long as you didn't get caught?"

"Maybe." He lifts his cup to his lips, and pauses, "But not livestock."

I laugh. I can't help it. Today sucked. "You're such an ass."

"I can't help it. I've got a naturally assy thing going on." He shrugs and smiles at me. Leaning forward he says, "Cheers, baby," and clinks his cup against mine. "Here's to you finding the perfect opportunity."

CHAPTER 9

A few more days pass and I know I'm killing time. I twist the card Miss Black gave me, eyeing the phone number like it has teeth. Nerves twist my stomach into knots. *Stop thinking*, I scold myself and press the digits into my phone.

Miss Black answers on the second ring. "Can I help you?" she asks.

I find my voice. "Apparently, you can. I want to know what's next, if I accept your offer." I know Miss Black knows who I am, that she expected me to ring her.

"Pictures, blood tests, and setting up a profile page is the next step. All of that is done here. Come in tomorrow night at 7:00pm and don't be late." The line goes dead.

I look at the phone cradled in my hand. This is my choice. I choose not to sleep in a box. I choose to keep a roof over my head. I choose to be a... Mentally, I pause. I still can't admit it, not even to myself.

I dress quickly and run out of the apartment before Dennis tries to talk to me. He's Amber's boyfriend, a short, stocky looking guy that flirts with anything that breathes. I can't stand him. The only person who irritates me more is Amber. I tug a sweater over my head and pull on my sneakers. I lace them, hopping on my foot and practically running for the door. Amber isn't here, but she gave her boyfriend a key. Of course, she didn't ask me. I try not to think about it and make a beeline for the door.

Dennis is standing at the kitchen counter wearing nothing but a smile. Seriously. Pants, man! Put some clothes on. He starts to say something to me. I don't look at him.

"Not now, Dennis! And I swear to God, if you don't start wearing clothes when Amber isn't around, I'm going to put crazy glue on your favorite seat and laugh my ass off when yours is stuck to the sofa."

"Harsh. I'm just—" he says as I slam the door behind me and cut off his sentence. The guy is an idiot. He flirts with everyone and everything, and to top it off, he thinks walking around naked should be a sport. Maybe it should be, but not for him and not in my apartment.

I'm dressed comfortably tonight. I have to hitch a ride to get my car. I'm hoping it's still there and the place didn't tow it during the day.

Mel picks me up downstairs. "Hey, you ready?"

I nod. "Yeah, I couldn't be more ready." I walk around to the passenger side and slip into her car. Mel starts the car and stashes her purse in the back seat.

"Dennis?" she asks as I buckle up and she pulls into traffic. I nod. "Naked?" I nod again. "That fool needs to wear pants."

"I told him that I'd glue his ass to the couch if he doesn't cut it out."

Mel snort laughs and cuts someone off. They blare their horn at her. Mel flips the driver off and bobs and weaves through the cars like a race car driver. "I bet he took that well."

"I didn't stick around to find out."

"Uh huh, and with good reason."

Mel drives me to my car. She looks around like she wants to ask me something, but she doesn't. The parking lot is about half filled. My car blends in, well, as much as it normally does anyway. Thank God it wasn't towed.

I slip out and thank her. "I'll see you later tonight."

"Good deal. There's a party at Mack's. You planning on stopping by?"

I shake my head. The wind picks up and blows my hair. I tuck a strand behind my ear. "Can't. Gotta study."

She nods. "You're not going to work tonight, are you?"

I shake my head. "Nah, actually I'm going to give notice. I've had another job offer and I decided to take it." I feel nervous and excited at the same time. If she wasn't beaming at me, I wouldn't have been able to say it.

Mel makes a high pitched noise that sounds like a squirrel being hit with a tennis racket. She bounces up and down in her seat. "You told Black yes? Ah! I can't believe it! Make sure to add goodie-two-shoes to your profile. Guys like that kind of wholesome— hey! What are you...?" I slam the door shut and smile at her. I wave my fingers at her through the window and hear some choice words through the glass.

"Yeah, yeah. I'll see you later, foul mouth," I say, grinning.

The window slides down. "Goodie-two-shoes is gonna be your new nickname."

"Funny. And I thought you'd go with something more classic." I smirk at her and she shakes her head.

Her hoop earrings sway back and forth as her mouth drops open.

"I'm saving those for later." Mel shoots a knowing look at me. It makes my stomach dip, like I have no idea what I'm in for. "When are they doing your kit?"

"Tomorrow night."

"I'm so coming!"

I fold my arms over my chest and tilt my head to the side. "Fine, as long as you don't make it weirder, because it's already weird."

"Yeah, I—" Mel's eyes fixate on something behind me. She stops talking and has a strange look on her face.

A familiar voice fills my ears and my body reacts. "Avery?" I turn slowly and see Sean walking up behind me.

Mel's eyebrows lifts so high they're about to slip off her face. "Is that—?"

I give her a look that says SHUT UP. "No."

Sean stops next to Mel's window and stands in front of me. "Long time no see, hot lips."

My face flames red. Mel's mouth opens, making an audible *holy crap* sound. I turn to her and tap my hand on the door. "Better get going. I'll catch up with you later." Code: Go away right now and if you say anything, I swear to God, I'll break your face.

Of course, Mel says something. "So, hot lips? Meaning you've already sampled the goods?"

"Something like that," Sean says smiling. I take his hand and pull him away from her car.

"Get your ass home, Mel. I'll see you later." I keep my hand in Sean's and pull him back toward my car, as Mel pulls out of the parking lot. I know she didn't want to leave, but I'm relieved she did.

Nervously, I jabber, trying to fill the holes in my head. I feel like I'm hemorrhaging words. They keep coming until Sean stops me. When I reach for my car door, he stops me, and turns me toward him. Reaching for my face, he tilts my chin up and looks into my eyes. I freeze. My heart pounds harder and harder. I think it might explode. A shiver slips down my spine.

Sean says, "There are very few things that captivate me as much as you do." His eyes drift toward my lips before lifting to meet my gaze. Butterflies fill my stomach. An insane compulsion to giggle washes over me, but I manage to subdue it to a smile.

"Insane compliments will get you insane answers." I feel the grin stretching across my face. "Let's keep our feet firmly planted in reality."

"All right. How about this? I have never, ever met someone that draws me in the way you do. It's everything—the way your hair sways when you walk, the curve of your hips at your thigh, the sound of your voice, the way your eyes dart away when I compliment you—like no one has ever told you how beautiful you are—everything about you is enticing. Like a moth to a flame."

"Ah, it's cliché time."

Sean touches my cheek with his hand, slowly slipping his warm fingers across my skin. My stomach twists into knots. I want to lean into him, but I don't. My eyes close as he does it. I can't hide how much I like his touch. His voice pulls my gaze back to his lips. "There are only so many ways to tell a woman she's beautiful. I'm bound to run into a few clichés from time to time."

I smile shyly, like I don't believe he finds me that attractive and turn my face away. It breaks the contact with his hand. I wish I hadn't done it, but I can't feel like this about him. He's going to be something else, someone else. This can't happen. I open the car door and slip into the seat. I dig the key out of my purse and stick it into the ignition and twist. I feel like I'm forgetting something. Sean makes my brains melt and I can't think. The car doesn't start. It doesn't even try to turn over. Ugh, slacker car from hell.

"You forgot the magic spray," he says softly through the cracked window. Sean holds up a can of ether and walks to the front of the car. He lifts the hood and sprays. I hear his voice a second later. "Now try."

I gas it and turn the key. The engine sputters to life. Sean walks back around to my window. I roll it down half way, where it gets stuck. Sean slips me the can. "I thought you might need that."

Smiling at him coyly, I ask, "Are you stalking me, Mr. Jones?"

Sean shakes his head and leans against the roof of the car. When he does it, he moves in closer to me and I catch his scent. It fills my head and I inhale deeper. "Quite the contrary, Miss Smith. I go out of my way to avoid you, however, you keep appearing right in front of my favorite diner at various hours doing all sorts of strange things. It's difficult to ignore you."

"Strange things?" I grin. "Such as?"

"You have a spray start car, for starters. That's not something I see every day. Second, you chased your car after getting it jacked, which was something, especially since you had every intention of getting your car back. When you consider that the car has no monetary value, it makes me wonder why you'd risk your life for it. And after much consideration, I've decided you've filled the tires with gold and that is the reason why you couldn't possible part with this beast, and it also explains why you go through ether cans like hairspray."

I blink at him. Am I strange? When did that happen? The image of using ether as hairspray enters my mind and I laugh like a hyena. "You pegged me, good citizen. Thank you for watching my golden goose while I was away at school, failing my tests. I shall reward you greatly." I'm joking, not thinking about what I' saying as I say it.

Sean's smile slips. "And what reward will that be?"

"You'll have to wait and see."

Sean straightens and steps away from the car so that I can pull out of the parking spot. I've been revving the car engine every few seconds to keep it running. Exhaust fumes fill the cold air, making white smoke.

He says, "I'll see you around, hot lips."

"Oh, you have no idea." Grinning, I pull my car out of the parking lot and head back to the dorm. I'll quit tomorrow. Right then, I felt so good and everything was going right for a change. I didn't want to mess it up.

CHAPTER 10

Mel asks, "But where did he come from? All of a sudden, I looked up and he was just there. Poof!" Mel makes imaginary sparkles with her hands, like she's a magician. "And correct me if I'm wrong, but he looks a little bit familiar. I would have sworn that I'd seen him somewhere before."

We are sitting in her dorm room. Her roommate is out and Mel is bouncing up and down with excitement. She walks across the room and flops on her bed. I sit in the comfy chair opposite her and pull my feet under my butt.

"Mel, I don't know where he came from. Sean seems to haunt that corner like a ghost. The first time I met him, he rode up next to me on a motorcycle and helped me get my car back. It was the night I was carjacked."

Her grin widens. "He's hot and he's chivalrous? Jackpot!"

I shake my head. "No, not jackpot. He's messed up. Sean looks familiar because his picture is in the book at Miss Black's. He was the one who wanted a virgin." I don't know what I think about that. He seems normal without that piece of information.

Mel starts to say something, but her mouth hangs open. It's like the words evaporated or something. I lift a brow at her, like *I told you so.* A snarky expression flashes across her face, "Don't go giving me that look. Everyone is fucked up to some extent."

"This one seems more so than others." A memory slips into my mind. I can see Sean's eyes and feel them on me. It makes me heart race. I hate that I have that reaction to him. And his lips... *Shut up!* I scold myself. I add, "Besides, most guys don't go looking for hookers."

Mel holds up a finger and corrects me. "Call girls, high priced call girls. There's a difference." Like I should know that.

I snort. "Yeah, meaning the guys have money."

"Well, that's a difference," Mel says like it's a valid point. She locks eyes with me and says, "So, let me get this straight. This really hot guy offers to help you when some asshole steals your car, you accept his help, you guys get your car back, and then what?"

I nod as she speaks, affirming her conclusions. "Then, nothing. We said good-bye. I don't have time to date and Sean didn't seem interested, but then I saw him again. And again. He brought me home last night after I flooded the engine trying to start my car." I have that vacant look in my eye that tells her that I'm remembering more than I'm saying.

"And…" she prompts, prodding me with her eyes.

I shrug, not wanting to tell her about the kiss. "And nothing. He's fucked up. You said so yourself. I can do damaged, but not—"

Mel starts laughing and I have no idea why. She's lying on her back on the bed and actually kicks her feet over her head and holds her stomach as she shakes with laughter. As usual, I have no idea what's so funny. Thinking quickly, I wonder what I missed, but don't see it. I throw a thick pillow across the room and it slaps into her thigh.

Mel rolls upright and wipes a tear from her eye. Still smiling way too big, she says, "Holy shit! That's why you took the job with Miss Black! You like him." She's grinning at me now. Suddenly Mel regains her composure. Seriously, she asks, "Tell me, Avery, what are you planning to do when you meet him as Miss Black's girl? Pretend that you're someone else?

Pretend that nothing ever happened? Or are you planning on using the SURPRISE! method of scaring the crap out of the guy? Ya know, cakes aren't part of our MO."

I rub a finger to my temple. I didn't really think about that part. "I thought he'd just gloss over it."

"You're kind of hard to forget. You seriously think he'll act like he doesn't know you? Who's mental now?" Mel folds her arms across her chest and gives me a look.

I make a strangled sound and bury my face in a pillow. Okay, maybe this is a bad plan. When I look up I say, "I am, obviously." I take a deep breath and ask, "What do I do with this? Who signs up for this and has sex with a guy that she already knows?"

"No one. There's a rule. Miss Black is strict with it. There are no extra relationships outside work when you're with her company."

"Why buy the cow when you can get the milk for free?"

Mel blinks at me. "What fucking cow? We're talking about you. White folks are so messed up." She shakes her head and looks up at me, totally serious. "If you work for Black, you have no relationships outside of work. There are no real names, no addresses. Everything is done at hotels. The entire point is anonymity and the guy gets whatever fantasy he wants fulfilled. You kind of messed that up since you already know him."

A jolt of panic shoots through me. I lean forward in the chair. "I don't really know him," I stammer, "I mean, I don't know his last name, where he lives, I don't know anything about him besides that he's hot and has a motorcycle."

Mel holds up a hand and cuts me off. "What, you think I'm gonna rat you out? Get real, *chica*. I'm trying to help you. Don't mention any of that to Miss Black and stay away from Sean outside of work. He knows the rules as well as you do. Besides, if he breaks them, I hear Black has a security team that breaks his legs."

"Are you serious?"

She nods. "There's a lot of money in this business, enough to keep us safe and keep the guys from turning into stalkers. No one messes with us." No one speaks for a moment. Mel's amber gaze lifts and meets mine. "Are you really going to do it?"

My voice barely comes out. "I have to. There aren't other options. Rent is astronomical and some temp job will render me homeless faster than I can blink. I did the math. I'm screwed. I might as well accept this as fate and go with it."

"Fate?"

I nod. "Yeah, if it wasn't him—if I never met Sean—I couldn't have gone through with it. As it is, I feel sick."

She smiles weakly at me. "I know what you mean, but don't worry, it'll pass and I'll help you through it."

CHAPTER 11

The photo shoot isn't what I thought it would be. There's a photographer—an older guy with a huge black camera—and Miss Black. We start by taking pictures of me clothed. They take a few headshots and then move onto full figure shots. I'm wearing jeans and a clingy sweater. I look young. My hair falls down my back in thick waves. They set my curls before we started the shoot.

I feel silly. That's the best word for it. I have trouble loosening up until Miss Black gets me talking. Then, things go better. I feel more at ease. I laugh. They put me in a few different outfits and the final outfit is a skin tight black dress. The back is extremely low and dips past the small of my back.

The dress is like a second skin. Every imperfection I have stands out and I feel like a fat hobo.

"This can't possibly look good." I say, pulling at the dress.

Miss Black swats my hands away and says, "You have no idea how stunning you are, do you? The dress fits perfectly, and what you think is fat are feminine curves. Without them you'd be a broom handle, so stop fidgeting and go sit over there." Miss Black points to a corner with a bench in front of a bank of windows. The city scape is behind me. The photographer moves his gear to the new location. It's the only shot that isn't on a backdrop.

I sit down and smooth the dress. I start to tug down the hem, but Miss Black, says, "Leave it. Turn toward the city, Avery. Look out the window and pull your hair over your shoulder."

I finally understand what they are doing. I twist toward the glass and flip my hair over my shoulder. It sweeps all to one side. I glance back at them. It's a more natural shot, like they're taking the picture of me when I don't know it. The photographer stands behind me with the camera to his face. I hear the shutter click. I glance at Miss Black for guidance, but she doesn't give any so I turn back to the glass. I lift my hand and touch the cold window pane with my finger, staring blankly at the city. I don't smile. I feel lost. My life is nothing like I thought it would be. I wish I'd gone with my parents that night. I wish I wasn't left here alone. I watch the red and white lights race by below. Life seems so fleeting, so pointless. I take a breath in and look back over my shoulder. The shutter snaps capturing the haunted look in my eyes.

Miss Black has her fingers on her chin like she's pleased. "Very good, Avery. You're done with this part of the kit. We'll do your blood work and fill out the rest of your papers."

I nod, surprised that there aren't more damning photographs taken. As if she could sense my thoughts, Miss Black says, "We don't do nude pictures. The joy of seeing the woman in the flesh for the first time is part of the package. The rest of the pictures are to give an idea of your personality, likes and dislikes."

"But you didn't ask me any of that."

"I know. You'll be the girl we tell you to be, which is very close to your natural inclinations anyway."

I nod. I don't care anymore. I change out of the dress and put my jeans and sweater back on. When we get to the paperwork that I saw the first time I was here, I don't know what to check off. I've never done any of it, so how am I supposed to know what I will do or won't do.

I'm sitting at the same small table at the back of the cubicles. The place is empty again. I wonder if anyone is ever here, besides Miss Black. I look at the paper and blink.

Miss Black sits next to me with a cup of coffee. It's black. She hands it to me. I sit up and take it. Miss Black pulls the papers in front of her. "I have an idea. Why don't we write on here that this sheet will be modified as experience is accumulated?"

"That's fine for future, er—dates, but what about now?" I ask.

"Treat it like a normal relationship and tell him when to stop."

"But if there are no hard boundaries…"

"You lose some of the protection afforded by the rules. I know what you're thinking, but it's impossible to know what another woman will like or what she won't tolerate. There are some things here that I thought I would never do, and that I've grown to enjoy." I must give her a weird look because she leans forward and touches my hand, saying, "Don't misunderstand. I want you to feel comfortable, so let's put a progression on here that way he can't skip to the kinky stuff without doing the normal stuff first. Is that all right?" I nod. This is so weird. Miss Black smiles and writes it on the paper. "Good. I think this lines up with Mr. Ferro's preferences anyway."

"Who?" I ask, wiggling to the front of my seat.

"Mr. Ferro, the man who I wanted to pair you with." Miss Black stands and retrieves the large book from the other night. She flips it open and it's everything I can do to *not* react. It's Sean. Pictures of Sean, his preference sheet, his description of what he finds attractive, and more. "Don't be afraid, Avery. It's only a binder. Take it and look."

I do as she says, and pull the binder in front of me. Mr. Ferro. Sean Ferro. There is no first name on the sheets. Miss Black explains how they only use formal names, that I am to call him Mr. Ferro. I wonder if that name is real or not. I wonder why he came in here, why a handsome man like Sean would want this. I touch a picture, looking at his eyes. My gaze drifts to his lips and I feel a zing float through my stomach. I blink hard to crush the memory and turn the page looking for answers, but there are none. It showcases a man that seems beautiful and normal.

Sean wrote that he prefers a woman with little experience so that he can take the time to teach her. What's that about? Altruism at its finest. He wants other guys to have better sex, so he teaches the new girl the ropes. That makes no sense. None of this does. There's a disconnect between this file and the guy I know.

A voice at the back of my mind says, *Maybe you don't know him at all.*

CHAPTER 12

My heart is banging into my ribs so hard that I think they might crack. I step out of the shower and towel off. Amber is screeching like a skewered cat as her headboard bangs into the wall. I so don't want to hear this, but I had to be home to get ready to go out.

I locked myself in our bathroom and put on my make-up after showering. I tie a bathrobe around me when I finish. Mel has a dress that she's lending me for tonight, since I didn't have anything suitable.

I think about seeing Sean, about what I'll say. Part of me thinks that I shouldn't say anything, that I should let him explain the whole thing. After all, we are both way more sketchy than we seemed.

Amber's voice busts my eardrum and then she finally shuts up. I try to sneak out of the bathroom now, before the two of them have a chance to start again. I toss my make-up back into my bag and run for the door. The way the room is situated has both our beds in the same area with a little Jack and Jill bathroom off of one end that we share with the girls next door.

I race by the beds and fail to notice the guy—not Dennis—standing in our kitchen. He has my throw blanket tied around his naked hips.

The guy looks up at me and then glances at Amber. "Hey, babe. Is this going to be a threesome? I'm down with that." He grins at me. The guy is a clone of Dennis. What the hell? I glance back at Amber, shooting her daggers, but she's lying in bed and doesn't bother to look at me.

"Don't touch my things!" I snap at him.

He grins at me like an idiot. Without thinking, I reach forward, snatch the blanket, and run out the door leaving the guy standing there with nothing on.

I run down the hall, holding the blanket between my fingers. When I step into the room, Mel seems annoyed, but her mood quickly changes to disgust when she sees the way I'm holding the blanket. She opens a drawer and pulls something out.

"Oh gross, not again." She holds up a trash bag for me and I drop the blanket inside. It'll need to be cleaned again and I don't want his junk all mashed up in my other wash.

"I don't even want to talk about it. I swear to God, she's the worst roommate ever. The only thing she's got going for her is that she doesn't steal."

Mel doesn't look convinced. "No offense hun, but you ain't got nothing worth stealing."

"Story of my life. So help me shake of the heebie-jeebies and get ready."

Mel snorts a laugh. Her hand quickly covers her mouth as she continues to laugh. "Where did you learn those words? You'd think you were raised in a nunnery. Damn, girl." Mel shakes her head and walks over to her closet. A dark violet cocktail dress is hanging at the front. She pulls it out and hands it to me. "What do you think? With your dark hair and eyes, I thought that color would work well for you. Plus it's easy to wear."

I hold the soft fabric in my hands. My heart starts pumping harder. I'm going to do this. The dress is the final step on the tightrope of insanity. I'm kind of hoping I fall off and break my neck. I don't know if I can go through with it. I nod, not saying anything I'm thinking. "It's beautiful."

The dress has a bright purple silk lining that is covered by black chiffon. The necklines scoops low and the back dips even lower. It's held up by a silver clip on one shoulder. It's like a Greek Goddess dress.

I blink at it for a moment. I can't believe this is happening.

As if Mel can sense my thoughts, she says, "And how about the rest? Did Mandy hook you up with a nice lacey garter set?"

The undergarments are inspected by Miss Black before I leave in a limo for my appointment with Sean. Nothing I had would have been acceptable, so I took what little money I had left and bought some stockings, thigh highs, panties and a bra. Everything was on clearance, but the whole thing is from a store on Miss Black's approved list.

I nod, and slip off the housecoat so she can see. It feels a little funny, but I have to put on the dress anyway. I pull it off the hanger as Mel looks me over. "There wasn't much in my price range."

"Well, I'm just glad they had something. That should pacify Miss Black. She just wants to make sure we don't skimp on anything."

"I can't believe how much this stuff costs. The stockings cost more than my entire outfit."

Mel shakes her head and smiles at me. "But have you felt them?"

"Yeah, they're buttery soft, but at that price I'll cry if I snag them." I'm trying to wriggle into the dress without messing up my make-up. It slips over me and I reach for the side to zip it, but Mel's already there. She pulls up the zipper for me and I look in the mirror. The dress fits perfectly. The bodice is formfitting and the skirt is on the shorter side and flares slightly at the hem. If I didn't feel like I was going to puke, I'd twirl.

"You look perfect."

"Thanks," I say, pulse pounding harder. I take a deep breath and try to calm down.

"Have you thought about what you're going to say to him?" Mel steps back and grabs a comb. She quickly pulls my long locks into a beautiful style. I don't even know what to call it. It's half up and half down. Loose strands hang by my shoulders as random curls are pinned and twisted onto the back of my head.

"No, not really. And Mel, if he says no, I'm walking away from this. If I can't do it with him, I just can't do it."

Mel stills her hands and presses her lips together. "You give up too easy."

"Maybe, but I have to be able to live with myself. My body and emotions aren't detached. I don't know how to do this without falling for the guy."

Mel folds her arms over her chest. She still has to get ready to go out later. "Listen, it'll come to you. One of the things I don't do is lingering kisses, you know the kind. They get all hot and heavy. It makes it feel like something it's not. That preference sheet isn't just what you like, it's what you can tolerate."

"What if I cry the whole time? What if I can't tolerate any of it?"

"You're stronger than that, Avery. Me and you, we're on our own. We're strong because we have to be. We don't need anyone or anything. We got our sights set on something and we get it, no matter the cost."

My stomach curls. She's just like me, maybe a little more battered by life, but we're the same. "The end justifies the means."

"Surviving justifies anything."

CHAPTER 13

I drive my crap car to Miss Black's. She invites me into the back and pulls out the measuring tape. I strip to my lacy undergarments and she takes it in, approves, and then measures me and writes it down. I slip the dress back on, careful not to mess up my hair and zip the dress up.

"There's one thing that you have to do to keep this job and that is to portray the confidence that our girls have. Since it's your first time, I know how you must be feeling, but all the same, you can't let it affect your performance. Because, that's what this is—a performance. The client wants an innocent young girl and you will fulfill that role. He doesn't want to hear your life story or why you entered this line of business. You are forbidden to discuss weighty matters or your personal life. Do you understand?"

I nod. It's not like I'm planning on spilling my guts to him and I can pull off inexperienced young girl, since I am one. "How am I supposed to be innocent and confident? I didn't think those things went together."

"Well, here they do. A tease is confident and younger women that flaunt their bodies usually have no idea what they're in for. You're to be that woman, confident and craving sex. Use your body the way you normally would to pick up a guy, but be more overt with it. Mr. Ferro will tailor the experience to be what he wants. When you get to that point, just follow his lead."

I nod again. It sounds easy, but I still feel my nerves swirling in my stomach. Miss Black asks me to follow her into her office. She rounds her desk and pulls out a gold bracelet from her top drawer. It has a little black stone in the center of the chain. She hands it to me. "Wear this at all times. It lets us know you are where you are supposed to be. If something goes horribly wrong, smash the stone. A security signal will be sent and help will arrive, but do not crush it unless it's life or death."

I take it and put it on my wrist. It's a little too big. "Has anyone ever had to use it?"

She shakes her head. "No, the threat is clear enough. Our clients know you have it and what will happen if one of our girls is harmed in any way. It's not pretty. The threat alone makes them behave."

I nod and stare at the black bead, wondering how it works. There must be something inside the stone, GPS and a transmitter of some sort.

After a few more words of instruction, I head downstairs where a car is waiting for me. My heart pounds against my ribs as I slip into the back seat of the limo. We pull into traffic. I feel like I can't breathe.

Calm down. It's only Sean. You can do this. My little pep talks falls flat. I'm afraid. I can't shake the feeling, so I try to ignore it. I look out the window for a while, but that makes me nervous too. I know where we are, I know where we are going. We'll be there any minute.

I decide to check my make-up. As I reach into my purse, the golden bracelet slips off my wrist. It's too loose. I look at it and know that I need to keep it on. Glancing at my ankle, I bend over and fasten it around my leg. It fits better there. When I sit up, the car slows and I see the hotel. It's one of the swank privately owned hotels in the affluent section of the city.

The car pulls in front and stops. My chest feels like it's going to explode. I don't breathe, I don't blink. The driver opens my door. I lift my foot and step out onto the pavement. Eyes fall on me, taking in my regal appearance. I wonder if they know why I'm here, and immediately dispel that thought. If they knew why I was here, there would be cops and there are none.

I step from the car and walk confidently toward the door. The doorman pulls it open for me, and I step inside. Miss Black told me to be confident, to move like I belong here, but my jaw drops slightly when I step inside. Opulence drips from every surface in this building. I try to ignore it, but I can't. My eyes drift from the gold gilding, to the large chandelier with sparkling crystals hanging in the center of the room.

I continue to walk. I'm to head to the restaurant on the second floor. I remember everything and when I reach the podium where the garson stands, my voice is steady. I am meeting someone. I tell him the name, and am led through the restaurant. The lights are low. The walls are decorated with rich fabrics and candelabras that match the large crystal fixture downstairs.

As I follow the man, I'm acutely aware of everything. Several sets of eyes lift and take in my figure before returning to their companions as I pass. I feel my heel strike the floor and the jolt through my body somehow makes me more confident. The tremble in my hands lessens and I hold my shoulders back. A soft smile lines my lips.

I think I'll be able to do this. I think I'll be able to pull it off. I feel perfect. I feel confident.

But then I see Sean. He's sitting in a darkened corner with his dark hair covering those blue eyes. He doesn't look up as I approach. His hand clutches a drink like it's a lifeline. The vibrant young man I met is gone. I can only see the shattered remnants.

The waiter stops in front of the table. I step out from behind him and move toward Sean. I lift my hand and press my finger to the monogram in the center of his plate. This is confirmation of who I am, so that there are no mistakes. Miss Black said it's our personal signal.

Sean doesn't look at me. The waiter pulls out my seat. I turn and slip silently into it and am handed a menu. I watch Sean the entire time. He won't look at me. Every piece of me wants to comfort him. Something is horribly wrong. I can tell.

We sit in silence until I think he'll never look up. Then, his dark head tilts back and those sapphire eyes lift and meet my gaze. Confusion flashes across his face at first, but it's quickly quashed by anger.

"What is this?" Sean growls at me, his voice low enough to not attract attention.

Fear wraps its icy fingers around my heart and squeezes. I no longer know what I want. I thought

Sean would be happy to see me, but he isn't. I don't want to leave him looking so betrayed, but I don't think I want to stay either.

"Hi," I manage, which is severely lacking.

"I repeat, what is this? Some kind of joke?" Anger surges in his voice.

"No," I say softly. "A coincidence."

Sean watches me, trying to sense the lie that he thinks I'm telling, but I'm not. "I'm sure," he says sarcastically. Shaking his head, Sean looks at me with venom in his eyes, "I thought Black wanted my business, but this is unacceptable. Go back to your boss and tell her the deal is off. I'll find what I need elsewhere. I don't condone her actions or being followed. I won't be manipulated." Sean stands abruptly. I know he's angry. He's going to leave. He's going to chew out Miss Black.

"Wait," I say, standing with him. I reach for his hand and hold onto his wrist. My voice sounds strained and quivers as I speak. "Please, don't tell her. She doesn't know. Sean, I know what it looks like, but please believe me."

His cold gaze cuts to my hold on his arm. I release him and take a small breath. "Why should I?"

"Because you're a good man and I need you to."

He stares at me for a moment and then sits back down in his chair. I return to my seat. He works his jaw as he considers me. "Explain, and don't lie to me."

I feel like I'm on trial. I want him to stay. I need him to stay. He's my last lifeline. Without him, without this job, I'm lost. My eyes dart away from his. "I'm not supposed to talk about me, but since I've already done something I wasn't supposed to—"

"Just tell me." Sean folds his arms over his chest. The waiter tries to come over to take our order, but the look on Sean's face scares him away.

I wring my hands in my lap under the table. Nervously, I say, "I need this job. When I saw your profile, I wanted..." I stumble trying to explain myself. "I thought it'd be nice that we'd already met. I haven't done this before, obviously, and—"

"I have trouble believing that," he snaps.

"Believe whatever you want, but facts are facts and you would have figured it out if I didn't screw everything up. Miss..." I bite my tongue to keep from saying Miss Black's name, "she doesn't know that I met you before, that I kissed you before." I stare into his eyes remembering that kiss, remembering the softness and desire. "She doesn't know, but I wanted to know you more, and I needed this. This encounter may not matter much to you, but it means everything to me." Before I realize it, my hands are on top of the table. I'm clutching them so tightly that my knuckles turn white.

Sean's gaze lowers to my hands and lifts to my face, "Why?"

I can't answer. My mouth fills with sand and I can barely swallow. All's I can manage is, "Please." I'm begging him. It dawns on me that this is what happened and I can't look at him. I release the death grip on my hands when he doesn't answer. Sean seems apathetic, leaning back in his chair as if he's dismissing me.

I take my purse in my hand, and heart pounding say, "I'm sorry. I won't trouble you again."

I stand and walk away from the table. Sean doesn't call my name. He doesn't stand and follow me out. He doesn't give me a second chance.

The limo isn't here yet. I'm on my own. My heart shatters as I realize what this means. Miss Black won't give me another chance, and I don't want one. I try to keep the tears from spilling as I take the walk of shame across the room. Stopping in front of the elevator, I press the button. I wait and take a shaky breath. When the doors open, an older couple slips out. They avert their eyes as is the custom when a stranger encounters a crying woman. I look at the floor as I step inside.

I lift my hand and press ONE. The doors start to slip shut. But just before they close, the door bangs against something dark that juts between them, a suited arm. The doors reopen and Sean is standing there. His blue eyes are filled with questions. He steps into the elevator with me. The doors slip shut. When we start to move, he pulls the STOP and the elevator darkens.

CHAPTER 14

His voice is in my ear. It sends a shiver down my spine. I feel exposed even though we stand in darkness. Sean speaks rapidly, "This isn't the way it's supposed to be. The rules were broken. I don't know what to do. I mean, I know you." I feel the heat from his body and know he's a breath away from me.

I'm not confident, but bold words spill from my lips. "Which makes it better, doesn't it?"

"No," he replies softly. "The anonymity mattered to me."

"I can't change that."

"But you changed the ground rules." I feel him lean against the wall next to me, like it pains him to admit it. "Now what? I don't want to send you back."

My palm finds his cheek. I turn his face toward me and feel his breath on my face. Softly, I say, "Then don't."

Sean takes a deep breath and suddenly the lights come back on. The elevator is moving again. When we reach the ground floor, I don't look at him. Sean says nothing. He takes my hand as we leave the elevator.

A person dressed in a hotel uniform approaches us. Sean swiftly walks past him without a word. I'm being led through the foyer and hotel staff and patrons are everywhere. Sean pushes through the front doors before the doorman can open them.

"Mr. Ferro, should I call for your car?"

Sean says, "No, thank you. Just taking my friend for a walk."

My heart beats harder. It's cold outside and I'm not dressed for it. I'm not supposed to leave the hotel. The little black bomb on my ankle will tell the ninjas to attack. After we pass the entrance, I dig in my heels and we stop. Sean looks at me with a strange expression on his face. I explain, "I can't leave the hotel grounds. She'll know."

Sean shakes his head and runs his fingers through his hair, grabbing at it. "This isn't turning out how I planned."

Although he seems to be talking to himself, I answer. "Nothing ever turns out the way I plan. It makes me wonder why I bother." Sean looks over at me. I grin sheepishly. "You caught me. It's not my life's ambition to be here tonight. I had other things planned, all of which got shot to hell. In a manner of speaking, you're my last chance...my last plan."

Sean seems surprised. His mood lightens a little. "Rule breaker," he teases. A light smile crosses his lips.

"Yup, rebel to the core." I answer. I sigh and suck in the cold night air and look around. People move up and down the street around us, all hurrying somewhere. I shiver and run my hands over my arms. "So, I can't pretend to understand your, uh, preferences, but if you want to swap me out—"

"No." Sean's eyes lock with mine. "You stay. I just have to figure things out."

"Why are we on the street?" I can't help it. I have to ask. I wrap my arms around my middle and try to keep warm. The wind blows gently, lifting the curls off my shoulders.

Sean looks at me. The expression says he can't tell me, and that something's tearing him up inside.

His spine straightens and everything changes. "Listen, we need a new arrangement."

"Agreed."

"But I need some things that came with the previous agreement. That's nonnegotiable."

"Fine," I say, shivering. "Let's go inside and discuss it like normal people."

"Since when are you normal? You run around with cans of ether in your pockets." He forgets himself and smiles. That hard mask he was wearing, cracks. My God, he looks beautiful.

The corners of my mouth lift. I step towards him. "Mind telling me why you were always at that corner?" I place a hand on his chest and smile up at him.

Sean shakes his head. "My secret." He's silent for a moment and adds, "You'll be safe with me, Avery, ah I mean, Miss Stanz."

Something flutters inside my heart when he says my name.

CHAPTER 15

Sean takes me to his room. It's the penthouse, located high above the city. The entire floor is ours. I've never seen such a place in person. Space is a commodity in the city and the vast size of the room is flaunting wealth.

"Do all guys get this room?" I ask, looking around. I feel Sean's eyes on me as I walk.

"I'd think not. It'd be a huge tip off. Plus the room cost more than the average services your company provides."

My face flames red. I try to hide it, but Sean sees my blush. He walks toward me and takes my hands from my face.

I say, "I've not done this before."

"I know," he says, his voice deepening as he speaks. Sean keeps a hold on my hands and turns me from the window to meet his gaze. A light dusting of stubble lines his jaw. That dark hair that I want to touch so badly falls into his eyes. He tilts his head to the side and it falls back. "Tell me something. How is it that you're a virgin? I wouldn't have thought that could be possible."

My gaze darts away from his, but he tilts my chin so that I can't look away from him. My heart is pounding rapidly and I feel vulnerable. I want to jerk my face away. I want to run, but I don't.

His voice is a whisper, "Tell me."

"I never found the right guy," I breathe.

Sean's eyes devour me, raking over my face like he can't get enough. Finally, he nods slowly. His hands drop from my body and I feel nervous again. I'm nervous when he touches me and more anxious when he's not.

Sean sees the slight tremor of my hand. He says over his shoulder, "I won't have sex with you, not unless you want it."

What? I nearly fall over. *Did he really say that?* "I'm sorry?"

Sean sits at a desk and turns the chair toward me. I stand in front of him staring with my lips parted. "It's the way I do things. I have no intention of forcing you. Actually, the whole thing is left up to you, really."

I swallow hard and stare at him like he has two heads. "But, I thought…"

"I know what you thought, but that doesn't matter now. We need a new arrangement, since the old one won't work anymore."

"Why won't it work?" I don't understand what he's thinking.

"Because I know you. It just can't be the way I thought, so let's come up with something new. I won't lay a hand on you, unless you ask me to. I won't have sex with you unless you want it. How's that for starters?"

"Sean, I can't change things that much. It isn't right. You wanted something when you called for me. What did you want?"

He's quiet for a moment. The fingers on his hands lace together between his knees as he leans forward. I think he's going to answer me, but he doesn't. "Listen, this week is hard for me, okay? I'm not usually here, in fact I do everything I can to steer clear of New York at this time of year. Business didn't work out that way this year. I need something to occupy my thoughts when I'm not at work, someone to be with. Since I know you can do that on some level, I want you around."

When he speaks, I hear the hitch in his voice. Sean's running from something, something he doesn't want to remember and being here forces the memory forward. I nod slowly and walk toward him. "So the arrangement is platonic? Not sexual?"

"Yes, if that's what you want."

My heart sinks. I look at him and I have no idea what I want. I thought I was going to have sex tonight. I nod, like I'm in shock. My gaze is lost, staring somewhere across the room when he speaks.

"That isn't what you wanted, is it?"

"I—" my mouth hangs open and I have no idea what to say. I try to explain, but I can't.

Sean looks surprised. "You wanted to do it, didn't you?"

I shake my head, but Sean puts his hands on my waist and pulls me to him. "You're breaking your rule," I say.

"I don't care," he says with a dark look in his eyes.

"Okay, then."

"Tell me what you want from this, what you want to learn?"

"Learn?" I squeak.

"Yeah, I'm assuming you felt safe with me and wanted to learn something. Isn't that why you picked me from the file? I'm sure there's more than one guy with a virgin fetish."

My heart is pounding. I can barely focus. I nod, even though it's not the truth. "Teach me," I hear myself say, and wonder how much ether I've inhaled. I must have rotted my brain.

"Teach you what, Miss Smith?" He holds me close, warming me. His hands linger around my waist as his eyes hold my gaze. My heart beats harder, faster. My face warms as I think about his hands on me, about what he's offering me. I wish I knew what he wanted originally, but I don't. I look at his lips, wanting to taste them, wondering what it would be like to be with him.

Smiling shyly at him, I breathe, "Everything."

~VOLUME 2 IS AVAILABLE NOW~

THE ARRANGEMENT SERIES

This story unfolds over the course of multiple short novels. Each one follows the continuing story of Avery Stanz and Sean Ferro.

To ensure you don't miss the next installment, text **AWESOMEBOOKS** to **22828** and you will get an email reminder on release day.

MORE BOOKS BY H.M. WARD

SCANDALOUS

SCANDALOUS 2

SECRETS SERIES

VALENTINE'S KISSES

DAMAGED

And more!

To see a full book list, please visit:

www.YAParanormalRomance.com/books.htm

CAN'T WAIT FOR H.M WARD'S NEXT STEAMY BOOK?

Let her know by leaving stars and telling her what you liked about THE ARRANGEMENT VOL. 1 in a review!

Made in the USA
Lexington, KY
20 July 2013